I Know What
the Small Girl Knew

Poems by
Anya Achtenberg

Modern History Press

Ann Arbor, MI

I Know What the Small Girl Knew.
Copyright © 1983, 2020 by Anya Achtenberg. All rights reserved.

Photograph of Anya Achtenberg by Michael Barich.
Photograph on Page 52 reprinted by permission of *The Guardian*.
Cover design by Jim Dochniak; photograph prepared by Michael Barich.

Library of Congress Cataloging-in-Publication Data
Names: Achtenberg, Anya, author.
Title: I know what the small girl knew / poems by Anya Achtenberg.
Description: 2020 edition. | Ann Arbor, MI : Modern History Press, [2020] |
   Summary: "A collection of juvenalia in poetry and prose on the subjects
   of social justice, women's rights, world conflict, and sexual abuse"--
   Provided by publisher.
Identifiers: LCCN 2020018327 (print) | LCCN 2020018328 (ebook) | ISBN
   9781615995172 (paperback) | ISBN 9781615995189 (hardcover) | ISBN
   9781615995196 (epub)
Subjects: GSAFD: Poetry.
Classification: LCC PS3551.C418 I33 2020 (print) | LCC PS3551.C418
   (ebook) | DDC 811/.54--dc23
LC record available at https://lccn.loc.gov/2020018327
LC ebook record available at https://lccn.loc.gov/2020018328

Grateful acknowledgment is made to the following publications in
which some of these poems first appeared: *Lake Street Review*, *Sez/A
Multi-Racial Journal of Poetry & People's Culture*, *Summit-University
Free Press*, *Sunbury*, *Quindaro*, and *Something to Say* (West End
Press).

Published by
Modern History Press   www.ModernHistoryPress.com
5145 Pontiac Trail   info@ModernHistoryPress.com
Ann Arbor, MI 48105

Tollfree 888-761-6268
FAX 734-663-6861

In memory of my mother, Rose Lewis Artenberg (1914 - 1993), and my father, Harry Artenberg (1911 - 1981)

for many friends, but especially Mary Joan Coleman, John Crawford, Jim Dochniak, Maya González, Jim Perlman, Paulette Jennifer Tabb, and the Boston Worker-Writers.

and for New York City, that wonderful monster that spit me out whole

Contents

FOREWORD

Anya Achtenberg's book is a collection of poetry rooted out of many, many years of history, a history that frames two continents. It is born out of the heart of a little girl who stands in the dark, remembering. She is the child of Jewish immigrants, but she could be the child of poor Blacks, Puerto Ricans, Chicanos, or Native Americans, a child of strugglers.

We are all born into this world by breath, a common originating point, and to use that breath to speak is a form of creating, and to go past that to where the voice sings means even more than survival.

These poems are a cry. It is a cry like weeping, mourning the pain of that little girl who looks out of the dark, the pain of nations, but it is also the cry of another sort, a song like the cry of a warrior who uses voice to call up memories that strengthen. Calls up the little girl into understanding. Calls up the grandmothers, the grandfathers, the oldest ones. Calls them not just for herself, but for us also, her listeners.

And she becomes strong, and so do we. And that is important, because we stand up.

— Joy Harjo

Author's Note to the 2020 edition, during the Covid-19 pandemic

The release of my long ago first book of poetry in a new edition, including an eBook format, is something I celebrate, perhaps even more so as I am in quarantine, as are many of us who can be. Serious periods of homelessness, living in homes where it was not safe, born from refugees, I have a glimpse of how much harder it could be for me at this moment. But for us with technology and a place to rest, eBooks are wonderful things.

How wonderful for this book to have had a foreword by Joy Harjo, who at the date of this edition is the Poet Laureate of the United States. In it, she says that the poetry is rooted in "a history that frames two continents". My understanding has grown since then: the ancestral journey across North Africa into the Iberian Peninsula, and centuries there under North African rule, must add a third continent tangled into these roots.

This book of my early poems is a kind of historical document indicating both the limits and the expansiveness of writing back then from a working class, partisan, traumatized consciousness, permeable to national and global suffering and struggles. What I did feel was how thin the membrane was between wars, between captivities, and how permanently ensconced the powerful seemed to feel. How much their art was taking; and ours, surviving.

It was written in "the good old days" of four minutes to midnight on the Doomsday Clock of the Bulletin of the Atomic Scientists—at this writing, that clock says 100 seconds to midnight.

What strikes me about my juvenilia, besides the uneven quality of the poems! is the clear class consciousness, the strong feminism, the connection to the human issues connected to race and racism. But when these poems first emerged, much of this was considered a liability by what passed as a poetry establishment; on the other hand, there were those who considered me a "diamond in the rough" they could mold into writing poems that made unequivocally clear political statements. That wasn't my work in poetry.

Because so many have done so much to make present and celebrated the literary work of writers from groups rarely represented when I began to be published, it might be hard to believe now, the pushback there was then, against poetry of class, race, gender, and international consciousness. But it was so in the United States. And writing this note in the midst of the Covid-19 pandemic reminds me how dangerous, even suicidal, is holding back the truth, or making expression in art only strategic or agenda-driven.

Regarding the title poem, "I Know What the Small Girl Knew"— I recall a middle-class woman at a reading of mine, also politically active, saying something to the effect, "Good poem, but it should show more of a struggle attitude!" Perhaps attitude was all. I had already been in the midst of serious struggles of my own, and united with the struggles of others. Many women came to me at my readings to thank me for expressing something of what they felt or had experienced. A few years after my acquaintance had imparted her criticism, I heard she'd moved back to the suburbs and ceased her activism. The poem aimed to speak to the lack of space in which to flourish for women, to earn, to access education; to find work that wasn't diminishing, demeaning, exploitive, sexualized. It did speak to the weaponizing of the male body, and, with it, sexuality; and the commodification of the female body, the young body. What I knew then, I haven't forgotten.

Why would I?

Anya Achtenberg
April 2020

Indeed I live in the dark ages!
A guileless word is an absurdity. A smooth forehead betokens
A hard heart. He who laughs
Has not yet heard
The terrible tidings.
                    — *Bertolt Brecht*

I.

For when she heard the explosion,
her eyes grew wet and wild.
She raced through the streets of Birmingham
calling for her child.

— Dudley Randall

what is this weeping?

what is this weeping she knows about? she is a child, she has not read the Bible, she knows none of the teachings, the history of her people. her parents do not speak of the past, not even of their life between pogroms. and she is a girl — she has not fought in the streets, had the *yarmulka* grabbed from the little dome of her skull. she did see "Jew Bastard" written on the inside of the kitchen cabinet in the apartment they moved into from the projects, but what, after all, are words?

and yes she has heard the piercing cry of the cantor, more a wail a cry a scream than a song, as it makes its quivering arabesques like those modern sculptures, bronze birds, flying to her cupped ears while she stands with her fingers twined around the railing among the women who speak of practical affairs, while their men sway beneath the padded shoulders of their gray suits, under the prayer shawls white with dashes of sky — the color one sees edging the trapdoor as one lies silent in a cellar.

is this weeping, this knowledge of weeping, a payment extracted for the sweet cakes she tasted after the service, or whenever anyone died or was married, or when the bony legs of her first cousin pushed him up to the rabbi to become a man?

* * *

why do her limbs fly out from her, always running, always dancing, and she cannot hold a small teacup but takes the bitter liquid from a glass? why do boots kick her as she works? and why do her ankles chafe when someone speaks of slavery? why does her face burn and her hands go to her belly when she hears that another black woman has been raped or murdered? why does the Ku Klux Klan ride into her dreams and put a rope around her father's neck, set fire to their small apartment, drag her and her older sister through the streets tied to the back of a horse?

and why does she still wonder if she is ugly, chewing on her fingers and grimacing before mirrors in the subway stations beneath the advertisements of skinny straight-haired girls?

she stares at herself, her eyes are some mixture, brown green the violet of some desert sands that shimmer beneath the hot dancing particles of wind, the gray green of the icy tundra, where some unknown sea has stopped

and she learns about weeping, and she learns about why

Survivor

the treadle rumbled
his foot pumped it
its black grillwork
spoke in a rumble
in the moving hieroglyph
of machine
in his shop in the bedroom
the needle vibrated
hitting its target
the bobbin whirled
and the treadle rumbled

deep in his throat
under loose skin, gray beard
his prayers rumbled
his half-closed eyes focused
on the precision of God — how He decided
who was bayoneted
in the shtetls of Russia
because his crimes deserved it,
whose books were burned
on the night of the Sabbath
because he didn't read them,
and whose wife was raped
because she didn't want
to remain faithful

Hymie knew
he had to stay away from his family
away from Sarah, the daughter,
whose copper hair had withered
as she watched for diseases
and cleaned the oven handles
with a toothpick,
away from the sons —
Michael the poet
dead of pneumonia at 24,

Jacob the cab driver
always at work
or in the sickbed
and Katie
the wife
whose brown flesh and Mongolian face
lured him
the smell of the old country
lingering
on her dark coarse hair
a sea to cross
back to where he whispered in Yiddish
and held her to his chest
until she warmed the straight bone
of his young back

and where
they were hiding
when the men
rode in
stabbing
the old ones
and the children,
running them down

* * *

at the end
he tried to hide
within the rumble of his prayers
from the sound
as god came to take him
while Katie's coarse gray hair
was weaving for him
a dream of their embrace
that ended with a rumble
exploding into pogrom

and the angular faces
of his mother
his father
and four tall brothers
 lost their ruddiness slowly
amid the laughter of horsemen
who held high the bloody organs
on the tips of their swords

and the trembling bushes parted
to his disbelieving eyes.

Autopsy

for Simmie Lee

In her apron pocket she keeps
photographs of her murdered son
taken after a police autopsy
was performed without her
knowledge, against her wishes

a man is marked by a giant X.
the lines skid
from each hill of bare shoulder
to each hill of gaunt hip,
they meet over the debris of his organs
to commemorate a pact
to bury an entire race.
his ten toes are still noticeable
to those who walked with him in summer.

the X indicates silence,
sewing the lips together
after the tongue is cut out.
i stare at the slashes that emptied him
his throat struggles to speak
his arms are steel beams
that fix me
like a roof above him,
my legs beat the air
and i stare at the X.

it indicates one who could not write
it lies in a territory invaded and pierced
with the sharpened end of a flag.
the funeral is not in my village
but my customs are similar.
i sleep beside the dead man's brother
in the dead man's bed.
his arms remind me of metal and wood,
his stomach cannot remember fruits,
it clings to the wall of his back.

there's a razor in your apple, child.

geography.
on this corner, an old man was killed.
cross the street and here a woman was raped
mutilated and
her body left in this lot
her clothing in garbage cans
behind this old stone building.
go three blocks and turn left.
if you're a woman
crouch down and
fold your arms over your breasts
for here a young girl child was molested
till the blood ran down her thin legs.
and if you've ever cared about a boy
or been one,
push your hands into the earth
at the edge of that park,
under the bent maple tree,
for here the last boy was found.

in Atlanta
parents lay out too many plates at suppertime
sisters notice there's more room in the bed
but after they're asleep, their legs run
they hunt all over town
in the darkness under the scratchy
army blanket.

even without a map
certain people always seem to know
where we keep what's most valuable.

for the children of Atlanta

it is about

it is about cars passing us
in the ugly weathers,
it is about planes overhead
as we walk,
it is about the terror in a body
that has been beaten.
i was paralytic, a captive,
a child who could not run.
it was only when i began to move
that i saw those who were kept still
backs bent in the fields
bodies hammered into rows
and understood them to be more
than my own reflection.

it is about an aimlessness
that is not pleasant
that does not end,
it is about an urgency
from which there is no release,
it is about a dream
that cannot be seen or even heard.
it is about fallen breasts and swollen legs,
it is the hoarse cry at death in the street,
the shooting behind the house,
the old mother who knows
he is better off dead
and yet mourns on her way to work.

it is about a child who does not grow
a fever that does not abate
a street that is impassable
a way that must be hunted
an escape that must be hacked out
from a proliferation of rubble
and dead eyes.

there must be a way to remove
the cruelty of ice from your bones,
there must be a way to remove
the spears of your mother's eyes
from your face, a way to remove
the knobby tentacles of your brother's fingers
from your arm, your brother who is dying
who has died as i speak.
there must be a way
to loose the hold without abandoning him
without forgetting his small fists of anger
his plans to set things straight,
without forgetting your conversations
soft and shouted
in the timeless circular light
of streetlamps in summer.

II.

and the grinding bad luck of everyday was
like a black cup that they drank, with their hands
    shaking.
                —*Pablo Neruda*

for Maya

i like it
that the onion is so familiar to you
as is the anonymity of rice
when the grains crowd together
with beans and hamburger
or cinnamon and raisins,
that the newspaper is shared
as is the exact location of a bargain,
and that our hands are not smooth
like pictures of hands in magazines
but rough, a bit bent already
and marked, like those that fed us.
and i like it
that our voices are filled with years
and have always been
since we were those very old children
you can always find
watching their classmates
wrestle each other
down to the ground

where we crouch
forgetting them
dividing our attention
between the small insects who work
long hours in the earth
and die young,
and our thoughts of history
its steady motion and convulsions
that we can't yet speak of
but which are constant thunder
in our small skulls
and a biting wind at our necks
as we huddle beneath our wild hair
at the bottom
of the enormous shifting sky.

to hurl a flesh arc

your own parents tried to throw you off the roof, 6 stories, shatter you like porcelain on the gray pavement, or strangle you with the heavy chain guarding the small patch of grass. even in death you would be forced to lie on the concrete rather than in that sweet green tickle, that cool earth that holds. no, it is hot and the pavement doesn't care.

they would throw you, hurl a flesh arc, a six-story scream — you! fling their refusal to watch you die slowly, a child without defense, no older brother, no dog, no strong fists, a slow-moving child with eyes pressed inside the head, eyes that blink and swallow each of the faces whose pinched mouths can barely speak, as you stand in the long waiting line for a little bread and milk and a bag of onions whose dry skins crackle in your hands like dead leaves under your feet.

so they would not have you wait in that line and receive the stale cottony bread, no hope of anything better. they would kill you instead, construct quickly and silently in the twilight, after he comes home from work, a flesh arc — no rainbow — that you must slide down, no child's plaything with a box of sand at the bottom.

you would shatter on the gray bumpy sidewalk that is lined off into squares — 2 of your steps can just barely clear one. i wonder how many squares will be needed to hold the pieces of your body. will a leg fall over a crack, then what misfortune? will they find your head, both eyes, what of your curly hair that some thought valuable?

and if you refuse, if you struggle? but no, they ignore it, the grim set walk, the strong hands not strong enough to give you safe passage out of your neighborhood that taunts bookreading.

they've become hard, they see no other way, so you pretend to lie shattered for years on the concrete, and the neighbors are sorry but have no time so hurry past. once in a while you etch a new line into one of the faces streaming by, whirling before your eyes like a painted scarf that fails to strangle you although your mother's red hands pull it tight around your throat to keep off the cold.

for many years they visit you. for many years you cannot look at each other. your hatred of them is a dark cloud floating up from the heart, but molecule by molecule it dissipates and waters the dandelions that grow around the chainposts. they stand before you, their red hands their hard hands behind their backs holding tears they've caught falling from rooftops. they step small circles around you, wanting a river to gently place you in and mend you to a whole strong body that can fight for them.

message from the Virgin of Guadalupe

on your knees to me.
scrape the skin to the bare bone.
your children run in front of you
with a blanket cut in 2 and sewn
a runner over the stony path
of your crawl. on your knees
to me, a picture of a woman,
because you are just flesh.
show your children their future
in your crawl to the church
i ordered be built,
show a bowed head to your children,
the children made by you and a man,
while i was only touched
lightly once by God
and bore your Saviour Jesus Christ.

crawl
on your knees
to my church
     that i did not build
     that i do not clean
     that i cannot fill with children
and i will show you my face
that does not change or age
while each December when you journey
to fulfill the vow you made
i see the lines in your skin
repeat themselves like tasks
and your hair is gray
and your back more bowed.

on your knees to me, woman,
for i am the mother of God.

December 14, 1979
Mexico City

so many of us come from this

i don't assume the dog
chained to the post at the corner
breathes
or that it will continue to
breathe
i stare at its belly
to make sure it swells and deflates
i need to watch the rib cage
changing in a rhythm

i watched my father's body
with the same purpose
as he slept on the threadbare rug
in the little box of a living room,
the little box we checked
what his income did not exceed,
the small box of what we could have
no skiing or jewelry, no getting away
the little box of a mirror
that disappointed my mother
when each time she dressed up
she never looked any more
like our one rich cousin

and the tasks
to sew to darn and buttons
the shoeboxes full of tasks
a cardboard box held the iron
the ironing board beat
against her legs
as she set it up,
the iron scorched peaks
into the shirts
into her skin —
mountains
for the eyes of a woman
who rarely saw trees

that i know music
is a miracle
that i have 2 legs
to dance
that the light does not ignore me
all miracles

what boxes do i know now?
the tables i wait at
papers scarred and papers blank
obituaries, help wanted
moving again, pack and unpack
looking for boxes
to open
i hear voices fly out
of everything i open

"get off the living room floor
what are you looking at?
your father's tired."
he never drinks
but the lights in the office
leave their flickering in his eyes
burn the soft brown there
leave red explosions in the white.
his back is a crooked yellow bone
but still they use it
his neck and shoulders disappear
he stops wanting
        sometimes only my mother's
        skin, it's not soft but
        warm under the bargain slip and
        panties, but she is always
        standing at the sink
        standing standing all damp from
        work and suddenly he
        wants her. they are hardly old
        we are kids but we

know, so he starts to rub
against her, hold her
round flesh. she is so afraid and
wants to cry, nothing in the house
is dry. there is pain and work and
sex covering everything so she
slips away from him, back to
work, her own overseer
and the flesh of her body shakes with
work, the frying pan from supper
the burnt pots
and she doesn't see his eyes fall
his head fall
the neck collapsing
the hands fall
empty
as he lies down alone
on the carpet that she vacuums
and his rib cage lifts
just a bit
and falls
falls

so many of us come from this

III.

What shall I do, set the landscape in order?
Set in place the lovers who will afterwards be photographs,
who will be bits of wood and mouthfuls of blood?
No, I won't; I attack,
I attack the conspiring
of these empty offices
that will not broadcast the sufferings

— *Federico García Lorca*

A Little Night Story

So again I hunt
beneath the dark jacket of evening
for the smooth chest
for the red drum inside
for its thin membrane
for the 2 soft patches
of a boy's nipples.
I look in my face,
there is nothing missing
except the breath of another
against it.
This is my current love story.
I sleep it off.
In the morning
there is work to do again
there is cleaning and breakfast

but there are also the eyes
and the open mouth,
the skin
and the long body,
its arms and legs
its thousands of hearts and sighs
its waiting
its childhood and its death,
no matter what.

the clerk speaks – 1
(Accounts Payable, East Boston)

"And you are earth swimming through the figures of the office."
— García Lorca

with this lipstick
the redness i buy and own
it looks like i have something
to give
it looks like i want something
i can use

something aside from work
something soft that dreams
something that remains in my body
after thought has gone to sleep.

i buy it
use it
dream
in front of the mirror,
my lips are
redder
than minus signs smearing
the long tape of
sums,
but after i
button my blouse
to the throat,
remove the flame
with a tissue,
my dry face is set
for the office

for stacks of invoices
that build nothing
for typing labels
that say nothing
for columns of numbers
that add up only for others

for the absence of flame
for the absence of dream
for the absence of soft
for the absence of love.

the clerk speaks – 2

(the IDS Building, Minneapolis)

i sift through papers
dream over machines
practice my poems
into telephones that ring
harsh so harsh
with the dying clipped
voice of managers.
this is the cleanest place i have ever been in.
i work   hour by hour
to eat   day by day
to sleep   a few hours
under the vast dream of night
i listen   to rats
behind the walls   i wake
to resent the sun   and the body
still dreaming next to me.
i go to pink message pads
groomed voices
the copy machine.

here i am told exactly what to do.
i sit at the desk
go mad with caffeine
touch myself like love
in the ladies' room

i eavesdrop
to the boss's
dry whisper
over the telephone —
he is arranging
for a woman to sleep with.
his voice swallows itself
goes down to his lap

he looks through the glass wall
over the city
he sees what he wants to
grab, suck dry and swallow
beat to a whimper
cover with his weight
take with his eyes closed

and never remember later
as he watches his small
and fragrant daughter
play in the soft grasses
of the backyard.

a work story

(For one year I worked with special needs children at a facility in Massachusetts. Aged 3 to 13, many were brain-damaged, often physically handicapped; others were geniuses and normal children in disguise.)

this last year, rising in the dark in the cold, constantly caring for children who cannot speak, who need to play tricks on someone, need to make long bloody tracks in the skin with their fingernails and i am close, i can barely defend myself for they are children and i cannot raise a hand against them. this last year of children who do not answer me but bang on the door, or try the knob if they know how, and sometimes i would be bleeding right into my pants and unable to leave them, or shaking with hunger but it wasn't time yet, and somehow i was locked inside with them.

o this year of telling children words that were ordered from inside the office, or sneaking around kissing them and whispering that they were beautiful and loved and making them laugh, until they remembered where they were and who i was supposed to be, and they would pull my hair until tears sat in my eyes, their small fists entwined in my ragged ancient curls.

at lunchtime inside their screams and the words of workers on the other shifts, i rested with my curls inside a mosaic, my veins and arteries were bright blue and red, and a whirlwind of smoke circled each eye as i looked out from the wall through centuries, watching the ways that children became deformed, watching all the workers

at lunchtime i stood in the kitchen and ate the leftovers from the children, swaying from one foot to the other, eating as if hypnotized or drugged. then, a little stronger, i talked to Maria who worked in the kitchen and cleaned up after us all, and her dark skin would glow and my curls revived a bit and stood up defiantly from my head, and then it was time.

then it was time to go back to work and the children clutched me again, or ignored me in their misery, hovering close to the wall, and the hours not the children beat me in the back and the legs, and stole my song away until later when it gently poked me with an awkward rhythm as i stood waiting for the bus and a sudden fresh wind caught my curls up in a dance and whispered to the back of my neck.

the clerk speaks – 3

(Columbus Circle, New York City)

for Bartleby the Scrivener, who died in prison. He was heard to answer, whenever his boss requested him to perform a task, "I would prefer not to."

i.   At my desk in the basement

oh my, my, my, I've got the Bartleby blues; I would prefer not to do these tasks, not to add up numbers for others and arrive at zero for myself, not to write up lists of what others possess, but I am held behind a desk when I'd rather be curled up in that space beneath it, hiding in the little shadow, so I depose the wastepaper basket and play turtle, staring at my fingers and toes as I pull them deeper into my belly and try to forget the bombs that have never left the swirly blue skies ever since they began to travel through.

I think about when they hit, and who made what in the deal.

my scrivening goes undone. I curl to a kernel, I am an acorn hiding from the squirrel; he demands too much and has the largest cheeks I've ever seen — a new breed I guess. I roll back onto the chair, I squint but can't make out any colors; it seems there is only gray, thick and cottony, dense flats dropped by means of wires from fluorescent lights that tamper with my optic nerves.

my hand astounds me. it grasps the pen just as it did in school, my back swayed since then, a proper clerk's back.

so I drop the pen and fall onto the desk, listening for music, a nice thing with sleep, but only a wheezing escapes the fan. its performance is not circular as in bars and old subways, but linear, a little tunnel hustling the smoke out into the streets downtown.

ii.   I try to look outside

where is the window? who has a view of Central Park? what ladies stroll through it? I can't. my dress, my hair, the worn look that is laughed at or run from.

they lean on the arms of, toss hair, smile with teeth and pink tongues glistening. they've excreted the wooly gray that starves the light and my pallor is worth noting for a moment, but they've danced by. they laugh and extend one finger, one finger only, hooked in an elegant lazy command, and the taxi comes to within one step of them, 1 up and they are through. safe. the seat is soft.

we run by the cab to catch the bus. this is a circus to them as they chatter in the back seat; we can't get so certain a vehicle. sometimes, however, a car comes right up to our door, sometimes a loud iron train into which we are placed upright hung on hooks or slid over heads onto shelves, each cold slab of us — we shake, and we remember. you have seen the tableaux, everybody has, remember?

iii.   The man and the woman climb the hill
      on the outskirts of Warsaw

> flowered dress, open shirt
> and his so smooth strong neck
> she has soft lips
> two clouds with hot rains between
> and jabs of lightning to his face
> his arms around her
> even then his hands tighten
> with memories of empty hands
> of sitting motionless right here on this hill
> and trying to take in the view
> but his head falls to the empty hands
>
> she leaps up and pierces the blue stillness
> she blazes against it
> she shouts
> raises her arms and dances
> and is happy but
> over and over again
> she shakes off disturbing visions
> covers her ears against the deafening
> clang of the iron doors

and he dance, she dance, dance
they take off their clothes and wash in the sky
with the sweet clouds
then fall to the ground
and roll and roll
and open each other to begin

but they've rolled too far
and the iron doors open
and they see they are naked
in the glare of helmets

he slows down and grinds stop
spitting earth and slowly rise
but the sky is a showerhead
that spits fumes
and she is gone

he crumples
and the hill watches
but now he is a little bowl of sweetmeats
and they pluck the rings
and his eyeglasses too
and he can't hear either

iv.   I get back to work

The subway hurtles through the darkness behind the wall. People walk
through the office, they are watching. My hand snaps back into place
and continues with the next item on the list. I curl like an old dollar bill
over the desktop. They approve of the roundness of my back, and move
on to check the next clerk.

IV.

tell me how i have become, became
this woman with razor blades between
her teeth.
            — *Sonia Sanchez*

the women

1.

the women who bear children alone
the women who were never children
the women alone at the bus stop
the women on the night shift
the women pulled into cars

the women who die in childbirth
the women whose children die
the women who listen to sirens
the women who wait at windows
the women with men in prison
the women who must hide

the women with red eyes
the women with no shoes
the women who can't speak
they talk to themselves
at the bus stop
                    the women
pulled into cars

the women who are raped
the women who apologize
the women who are beaten
the women who wait for men

the women called prostitutes
the girls called tramps
the women who cry in bars
the women who wait for men

the women who are fat
the women whose legs are scarred
the women with swollen feet
the women with red eyes

the ones who wait on tables
the women in the fields
the women who make soup
from bones
         the women
who fight with bottles

the women who listen to sirens
the women who work at night
the women pulled into cars
the women
the women

O the women who escape

2.

the women in the suburbs
the women in the sauna
the women at the salon
the women at the spa
the women are swimming
the women are tanning
the women playing tennis
the women

o the women with soft skin
the women who wear gold
the women who know silk
the women

the women with cleaning ladies
the women who cross
and uncross their legs
the women who don't work

the women who sit behind restaurant windows
the women whose teeth have no edge
the ones who hold glasses delicately
the women with faces of glass

the women who never work
the women who live in bed
the women with soft skin
the women who wait for men
the women in the back
of limousines

the women owned by rich men

the president's wife
the candidates' wives
the boss's wife
the landlord's wife
the women
the women owned by rich men

the women who laugh behind their hands
the women who sleep till noon
the women who wait for men
the women who drink too much
the women, O

the women
the women owned by rich men

3.

the women who escape
the women

the women who can speak
the women

the women who open faces
the women who do not serve
the women who fight in the river
the women who make words fly

the women who shout
the women!

the women who are not slaves
the women who led slaves to freedom
the women named Solitude
the women named Harriet
the women named Carlota

the women

the women who fight in the river
the women who do not serve
the women who can speak
the women who can love

the women
the women
the women

O! the women

The Mirror Woman

The mirror woman
is really flesh
but her blouse is all mirrors
curved ones for sleeves
two triangular mirrors
make her neatly pressed collar
little moons of mirrors for buttons
repeat you if you look
and the skirt, all mirror,
blurs you
almost drowns you
it gives you back so liquid.

After work
she gets dressed in mirrors
takes a taxi to the east side.
The driver peers into her
notices the sunburn on his left arm
resting on the side of the auto.
She asks him to let her out
pays him in ordinary currency.
The soles of her shoes reflect
each step on the pavement.
Cats follow her
studying their markings.

The rich, all nervous,
throw things to shatter
the image that repeats
in each shard of glass.
They throw pendants
old coins and spoiled fruits
whatever
they don't want anymore
until she is naked.

It relieves them
to see the tiny shark fins
enter her.

Ramona

(a painting by Gauguin)

it wasn't gauguin
but you, Ramona,
gave me back my breasts
full and longing toward earth,
my thighs brown and soft
around harsh bones,
dressing up my death with flesh
for the festivities of life

while the painter's violet
broken veins
pulse below the skin
erase one more heartbeat
he keeps count with
each brush stroke
puts the score
into a frame
and tries
to sell it.

> she gets up from her
> painted stool
> unpaid
> goes with uncounted steps
> to the world
> outside

> she locates her sky
> the fruits
> that open her mouth
> the warm bones of her people
> their throats their song
> drown the rasp
> of canvas ripping
> thread by thread
> in the high-pitched wind
> of time.

Stauch's Bathhouse

the lockers hold shadow
each woman comes from
      her cubicle of shadow

they unlace corsets
peel off girdles
unhook themselves
      breasts flow
      like long brown hair
      to hanging bellies faithful to
      the last child

one woman stares in at me
her silver hair folded into her
scalp, she holds a bottle
of blue oil, like a bottle
filled with sea
the Mediterranean
in her brown fingers
      she oils her skin
      follows the waves in her
      flesh

she stares at me
in my little body
      the insides of my thighs
      just beginning to swell
      yet unbitten
      the elastic of
      the bathing suit
      rides up them
she stares at me
as i hurry with the suit
strain
to untangle the straps
fit the top over
the new little hills

she holds up

a bottle of blue oil
the seas
rise over her, she shakes
the silver out
she shakes her hair out
like a girl dancing
in the sun, the sweat
runs from behind her ears
under her chin, glides
between her breasts
disappears
beneath the pouches

she rubs her breasts
with the blue seas, the long
brown nipples point
into her
belly, into the earth

she stares at me
i give a long shiver
in the chill of the locker
where cold sand gathers from all
who have slapped the towel
against the soles of their feet

i tie the thin straps
around my neck
take the key on its elastic
riding around my wrist
i leave her
in the wooden corridor
i run to stand
before the blue ocean
its silver foam
i watch the waves rise up, rise up
and throw themselves
into the cold sand
beneath the waters

Summary of Attacks at 4, 17, 23, and 28

i.

Four years old, doctor had to chase me out into the waiting room to
make me take off my undershirt, jabbing the ice of his instrument
against my flat breasts and tiny nipples.
Perhaps the thick rubber eels of the stethoscope were aiming for my
small neck.

ii.

He locked the car doors, rolled up the windows making it soundproof,
tore at my skin as he tore at my clothes, ripped at a mythical membrane
i finally understood i had had all along.

iii.

I sat on his thick leg, allowed his meaty fingers to play.
He pushed his leg further into me, further, so that my thoughts stopped.
I began to cry to make him stop because i couldn't speak.

iv.

He pushed me down to the ground, i couldn't see his face but
remembered it from down the street where i knew he was going to try.
I couldn't scream but only work, work to keep him from knocking my
head on the concrete again, work to take away his hands that moved
and multiplied all over me. He was silent, i couldn't scream or didn't
hear it if i did, all i heard was a long wind blowing down deserted
streets from a hidden throat long silent, until it pushed him off me.

44

I Know What the Small Girl Knew

for Meridel Le Sueur

red
against white
a shock.
blood
against the pale
gown.
my childhood fears were all true.
some men treat murder like a movie:
they pose, guns at hips
they charge into action
make one quick slash on their gun
for each good hit. we
sit behind the rocks
wash up the blood
on reddening knees. we
wait behind the trees
cry over our children, our mending.
I hear we were warlike
sometimes, but I have
no time to remember. I got
so busy watching the battle
providing a hiding place
not understanding why
my father was always cold
my lovers brutal.

* * *

the fears of a girl are all true.
seven boys in the alleyway
a man in the parked car
the dark suit bulging
laughter, the thudding
of ball playing
the flat hand that slaps
fists and the curses

the empty bottle and the beatings
locked in her room.

        * * *

a young woman does not forget
what the small girl knew.
I made plans for the weekend
a new dress, the dinner, seduction,
but I was seized
by the speed of the world unraveling
life after life.
I knew that time was demanding
a statement, a theory, a plan,
but I had never
never been asked before
I only stood at the door
over chess games
behind counters
silently swimming around
in my place close to drowning
pink flesh to yellow
in the dense gray-blue.

        * * *

I watch your conversations.
you pretend that I know
the meanings of the words
murder and power,
but you make quick waves of the hand
when I open my mouth to reply —
my blood spread too
seeped through the fibers
of the pale gown
when you shot me,
but I am still busy watching
not understanding why
watching the red leave
the surface of my skin
the tips of my fingers

under the nails
the lips
the earlobe in the cold
the old scar from the kitchen knife
and I don't know whom to fight
or where to go to get back my life.

* * *

I sit up in my bed
on high slippery peaks
over black oceans.
I know what the small girl knew.
I have read your instructions
heard your thousands of years of suggestions
I feel your hard fingers pushing
me to do
what you say
dying is.
you whisper of the one way
the way of death
as blood leaves the face
the legs turn outward on the table
the breasts offer no resistance.
I never understood your terms
your stopping at the body
fashioning it to a weapon
a knife, a pistol, a tank.
I left long ago
and childhood fears must all run away
even as the gown turns red
the skin below it pale.

* * *

I think
life and death will go to sleep
in my body, remain in my bones
in my dust on the hillside
while I wake
repeatedly.

V.

This is not hell, it is a street.
This is not death, it is a fruit-stand.

— Federico García Lorca

a small history of a large debt

in the projects of brick
the color of old blood
blood gone back to earth,
earth without root in the ancient core
of earth,
we hovered on landfill
behind frightened windows
watching for the shatter of seagulls
the manila shade turning forever
on its wooden axis
the pullcord bobbing
like a wild hungry noose
after the attack of birds on glass

we hid in 4s and 5s
some dared conceal more
in the middle of the century
after the war
and during the many wars
that raked many bloody furrows
over the earth
so we knew the soft blues and greens
of the maps folded into textbooks
were lies,
that this absence of crimson
was a lie

we all suspected the ovens
that glowed like moonrock
in the dark night apartments
and we could smell gas on the skin
of Leibowitz and Kaufman and Gorsky
we strained to see the purplish numbers
aging behind the graying hairs of men
about to ride the subway to work,
incalculable quantities
under the dark heavy sleeves of women
carrying paper sacks from the grocery

in the projects
there were concrete and grassy fields
or rather 1 field in the center
of 7 buildings,
1 field
enchained
but velvet
a feathery rain
bathing our feet
for an instant
1 instant
until the guards chased us away

in the small room
were cots filled with daughters
who slept above linoleum
the colors of the fields
many shades of green
like the many seasons side by side
as if we could see time
from an immense height.
our mother wouldn't let us shut the door
perhaps she wouldn't hear us
strangling in our sleep,
perhaps our dreams spoke evil of her
and she had to know

at meals no one spoke
we were rarely all together
we ate different things
we didn't like the eyes of each other
as we ate in fear
needing the food in our mouths

after schoolwork, the hallway
trapped us.
we traveled from the locked door
with its hidden viewer and safety chain
to the bedroom window with its green sill

over black asphalt with red streaks
passing the boots on the newspaper drying,
the undershirt hanging by its straps
on the penny-colored doorknob,
the scuffed baseboard and our own fingerprints
caught on the cold walls as we slid by

i am counting these years in the hallway
behind the open door that scraped my sleep
between the damned lying pages of books
in the schools built as well
of dead drying blood
i am counting the drops.
i am counting the years stolen from me
adding them to the number of families
in the projects
and how many children in each,
adding them to the number of wars
the numbers on the arms of the dead
the number of guards
minus 1 instant of spring,
the number of cots
and how many children in each,
and the number of walks stopped
by the dimensions of a dark hallway
or the dimensions of a prison cell
and i say incessantly,
so that some find me repetitive,
we are owed great numbers of things
and we will collect.

War and a Very Old Woman

She sits in the chair with the broken back
and sews.
She sits in the chair under tattered light
and sews.
She is sewing hands
back on their arms,
sewing.
She is sewing necks and heads
back on their shoulders,
sewing.
Then each toe
with many tight little stitches
back in their places,
sewing.
And with one
miniscule tack
in the center of each black pupil
she replaces the eyes,
sewing.

She sits in the chair for ten years
under tattered light for ten years
she sits in the chair with the broken back
and sews.
The troops
march around her feet
bayoneting the earth
shooting at her heels,
she sits in the chair
with the broken back
and sews.

She is sewing her son together
in the fiery light
the exhausted light
she is sewing her son together

Till the island spills its captives
and she wraps her arms around him
for the thread was strong and the stitches tight
oh she wraps her arms around him

Cassinga

site of a massacre of 1000
Namibian refugees
by South African forces

Cassinga
a mass grave
Cassinga
who dug it?
Cassinga
who filled it?

Cassinga
release your dead
to march over the earth
Cassinga
swell our forces
with each dead one
flung over each
living body

we live
in the shadow of Cassinga
inside our skin
the bones of Cassinga
reddening our fury
the blood of Cassinga

Cassinga dead
walk with us
the dead and the living
both live

Cassinga
a mass grave
Cassinga
erupting
the struggle
continues
Cassinga

Cassinga

La Prisionera

It's Lolita Lebron
her thin set face behind the bars
that try to imprison even her eyes.
With one eye
she looks to her island
with the other
she keeps watch
on the monstrous cities
              where her people touch home
              in bruised fruits crowded together
              in splintered crates
              leaning against the avenues
              bordering Manhattan

She looks to the strength of her people
              behind the racks of coats
              her brothers push down
              Fashion Avenue,
              in the fingers that push cloth
              under the unrelenting stab
              of needles —
              her sisters sit in rows
              in buildings still not safe
              from fires —
              and in the soft voices of children
              who wait hungry and sleepy
              to finally stand up
              little men and women
              and translate the words
              of impatient officials
              behind their desks at welfare
              and unemployment
              while their mothers' faces
              nod anxiously
              searching for rent money and food
              in the voices of their children
              speaking English.

Lolita Lebron
looks out over the padlock
draped with the bloody flag
of the United States,
the flag drenched
in blood of mothers
who can no longer be mothers.
She hears their cry
but in it
remains the Cry of Lares.
She looks to her comrades
        2 in Leavenworth
        1 in Marion
        1 dying
        then dead of cancer —
        the cancer he did not create
        it never belonged to him,
        never defeated him.

Behind the glass of the library window
Lolita Lebron watches the people passing by
watches especially the children
who sometimes stop at the library
the children who
so young
speak 2 languages
switching from one to the other
as they need to
while down the street
at the Big University
        the self-assured students sit
        in soundproof rooms
        earphones over their small
        ears and repeat
        over and over again
        in many languages
        "Where is the restaurant?"
        and
        "How much does this cost?"

Lolita Lebron
Oscar Collazo
Irving Flores
Rafael Cancel Miranda
and the struggling spirit of
Andres Figueroa Cordera
stand now in their freedom
that they never begged for
that they always fought for
among crowds of people
millions of people
in New York and Chicago
where people wait
with their arms outstretched
to hold them when they stop
for a while.

And their strength stays with the crowds
after they continue on their journey
home
to finally stand on the soil
of their country
that is still on the road to
freedom
and so close
to it that they smile
and smile
to the crowds that surround them
everywhere in Puerto Rico

a nation that must be
free.

four minutes to midnight

the time according to the Doomsday Clock
from the Bulletin of the Atomic Scientists
February, 1981.

1.   at breakfast

        the clock over the counter
        moves closer to midnight
        the kids discuss nuclear war
        spoon in the sweet
        cereal
        they've drowned
        in a milk that glows
        they lick the spoon, bite
        the metal, they need
        something

        as they read,
        the special offer on the back of the box
        is imprinted
        on the smooth little foreheads
        and a nude woman runs
        past my eyes, her dark hair
        a flame, her skin
        covered
        with branches
        and delicate
        black blossoms

2.   in Times Square

        the glass ball is dropping
        the happy musician dances onto the balcony
        they've hired him
        for the last big party
        before the weather changes.
        his blue shirt tugs at his belly

he is the man
who plays the great wooden fish.
he sees the dancers gathered
licks his lips.
he throws his head back, his mouth
swallows stars, they swim like small fish
into the big fish mouth.
his arm will strike, it
speeds up
gathers strength

the dancers in the square
scream with delight
beer cans roll
over asphalt, skid and crash
into their ankles, children
push each other down, glasses
hurtle through space
the great stick journeys
to the fish, how its scales glow
as it lies stiff in his hand
waiting for the blow
to send out its song
to the dancers.

he watches the fish
take the thud
on the thin skin
of its spine.
the whole plaza is lit up
the dancers fling their children
into the loudest sound ever heard
the children curse
they try to see everything
they are going to miss
but their own skin's glowing
too bright
and they can't cover their eyes
with their hands

everything is
too hot.

3.   that song

    that rhythm of the
    fish, its scud scud scud
    the tsa tsa the tsa the scud
    the fish that sings, it hums
    the low sound of fish
    in its little wooden house
    now the rivers are dry
    poison, listen,
    listen to the song of the
    fish in the air as it
    dries in the hand as it
    repeats the blow to its skull
    listen
    to the scaly rattle
    that lonely musicmaker
    who can keep us dancing
    just a minute longer.

no matter

for Paulette

When I became an old woman
with a rock at my left shoulder
and an aged bloated dog at my right,
with the rasp of a chain
for a voice,
with a hundred legs
all swollen and painful,
I moved with the slowest motion
that is not death,
I crawled beneath the conqueror
and saw that he does not dream
but uses the same words every day.
I counted the beats of my own heart,
figured out
I would outlast him,
and rejoiced.

You, who shall emerge from the flood
In which we are sinking,
Think —
When you speak of our weaknesses,
Also of the dark time
That brought them forth.

— Bertolt Brecht

Notes on the Poems

Part Two
"message from the Virgin of Guadalupe":
I lived in New Mexico twice, for a decade in total, where the gracious and loving Virgin of Guadalupe did indeed watch over me. This poem was written years before that, not about the dear protective mother, the Virgin of Guadalupe, throwing her exquisite light over her many children; the indigenous mother to whom so many are devoted. It was written rather from my earnest heart that knew little of that mother, but was in solidarity with those who so needed help they did indeed crawl on their knees for miles, bloodied and exhausted, out of that hope for the basics in life they surely had a right to...

Part Three
"the clerk speaks – 3":
Bartleby the Scrivener inhabits Herman Melville's short story by the same name.
"Playing turtle" was what the teachers called hiding under your desk at school to practice safety measures in case an atomic bomb was dropped nearby.

Part Four
"the women":
Solitude was a slave in Guadeloupe who joined many others in fighting for freedom in the early nineteenth century. *A Woman Named Solitude*, by Andre Schwarz-Bart, tells her story.
Harriet Tubman, "the Moses of her People," led hundreds of slaves in the United States to freedom by way of the Underground Railroad.
Carlota led a slave rebellion at the Triunvirato Mill in Cuba in 1843. The rebellion, as so many, was a failure, and she and all the rest were killed immediately. But she is honored by the Cuban people. See Margaret Randall's book, *Carlota: prose and poems from Havana* (New Star Books).

Part Five
"War and a Very Old Woman":
The photo is of a woman united with her son after his imprisonment for ten years by U.S. forces on Con Son Island, Viet Nam.
"La Prisionera":
The mothers who can no longer be mothers are the 35% of all women

of child-bearing age in Puerto Rico who had been sterilized (at the time of the original publication); some pressured into it by doctors and welfare officials, others without their knowledge.

The Cry of Lares — *El Grito de Lares* — refers to an uprising in September, 1868, against the Spanish colonizers who held Puerto Rico until 1898, when the United States stepped in. The town of Lares was taken by the patriots, and the "Republic of Puerto Rico" declared, before the revolt was brutally crushed.

The Puerto Rican Nationalists were the longest-held political prisoners in the western hemisphere until their release in 1979 (and Cordera's death the previous year). Collazo had been imprisoned since 1950; the others, since 1954.

About the Author, 2020

ANYA ACHTENBERG is an award-winning author of the novel *Blue Earth*, and novella, *The Stories of Devil-Girl* (both with *Modern History Press*); and poetry books, *The Stone of Language* (*West End Press* 2004; *MHP* 2020); and *I Know What the Small Girl Knew* (*Holy Cow! Press*; *MHP* 2020). Her fiction and poetry have received numerous prizes and distinctions, and been published in numerous literary journals, including *Harvard Review; Malpaís Review; Gargoyle; Tupelo Quarterly; Hinchas de poesía; Poet Lore;* and many more. As of this re-release of her first book as an e-book, Anya in quarantine is close to finishing *History Artist*, a novel-in-progress centering in a young Cambodian-African American woman, born the moment the US invasion of Cambodia begins.

Anya is a writer's consultant and unique teacher of creative writing, in-person through universities, writer's organizations and conferences, and privately through Anya's *The Disobedient Writer School*; and online, reaching 60 countries and thousands of students to-date.

Anya's teaching on writing craft goes beyond conventions with creatively expansive approaches that reflect multiple experiences, histories, aesthetics, uses of language, and approaches to story. Her essay on out-of-category identities and their relationship to the inadequate instruction to "write from a sense of place" was published in *How Dare We! Write: a multicultural creative writing discourse.* She has begun work on volumes that collect her radical creative writing pedagogy and workshop materials, including her *Writing for Social Change: Re-Dream a Just World Workshop* Series; *The Disobedient Writer Workshop Series*; and *Body Stories, Body Song, and the Elements of Story Craft*, informed by the many kinds of bodies, such as the captive, the liberated, the traumatized, the adorned, the dislodged and diasporic, the body in resistance, in a way that opens and shifts the writer's relationship to the craft of story.

Anya has organized a number of arts and history-focused multicultural journeys to Cuba, and worked to curate Cuban film festivals. She never forgot that it was in Cuba, after being asked what she did or loved to do, and responding, shyly, that she loved writing poetry, the questioner addressed her always afterwards, as "Poeta!"

Anya's forthcoming Patreon.org page will make her workshops and writings more widely available. Her courses, webinars, and critique groups are gathered at Teachable.com

For more information, please visit Anya's website, *The Disobedient Writer*, here: **https://thedisobedientwriter.com/**

Anya Achtenberg, original publication photo

"Poignant and fierce, this book is moving, beautifully written, and urgently relevant."

"Devil-Girl's stories are all of our stories, all of the 'discarded and demonized', all of us who have had to fight to survive, to fight to tell our truths. Achtenberg's wise survivor, Devil-Girl, is witness and seer, and her words are sustenance. There is much pain in this book, much wisdom, and a kind of beauty that sears itself into memory, a fierce beauty that is as necessary as air. Read this book."
—Lisa D. Chavez, Author of
Destruction Bay; *In An Angry Season*

"Achtenberg is a cutting-edge voice in the literature of the postglobalization age, an era in which we are uprooted geographically and spiritually, and redefining what it means to be home. What a superbly written book! Read it and be changed."
—Demetria Martinez, Author of *Mother Tongue*

"Stunning and original! Powerful 'make it new' language that creates-through the runaway energy and precise detail of the storytelling voice—a disturbing world in all its particularities, only to transcend it by grappling with what's at stake in the larger world."
—Stratis Haviaras, Founder and former editor of *Harvard Review*

"An amazing piece of bravura writing! Devil-Girl takes us from destitution to seedy glamour as a homeless vulnerable young woman tries to survive the savagery of the streets. Poignant and fierce, this book is moving, beautifully written, and urgently relevant."
—Kathleen Spivack, Author, Director: Advanced Writing Workshop

paperback * hardcover * eBook

ISBN 978-1-932690-62-0

www.ModernHistoryPress.com

Blue Earth is a compelling novel of Minnesota, a land that guards its secrets. Carver Heinz loses both farm and family in the farm crisis of the 1980s. Displaced into urban Minneapolis, he becomes obsessed with Angie, a beautiful child he rescues from a tornado in an encounter he insists they keep silent. Her close friendship with a Dakota Indian boy fuels Carver's rage and unleashes a series of events that reveal the haunting power of each character's past and of their shared histories, especially the 1862 Dakota Conflict and public hanging of 38 Dakota--the largest mass execution in U.S. history.

"We... see our own lives reflected in *Blue Earth*'s dark mirror, even as we learn a tragic history kept from us by those who would forever erase our origins... This is a brilliant novel by one of our truly intuitive and accomplished writers."

—Margaret Randall, author of *Ruins*

"Achtenberg's passionate, brilliantly crafted language, combined with her profound ethical imagination, makes *Blue Earth* one of the most important books to appear at this moment in our history."

—Demetria Martinez, author of *Mother Tongue*

"Achtenberg creates morally complex and culturally diverse characters whose lives are affected by loss, poverty, disease, and war, but whose ultimately redemptive encounters with one another take *Blue Earth* far beyond its Midwestern setting."

—Martha Collins, author of *Blue Front*

"In the great tradition of Willa Cather and Wallace Stegner, Anya Achtenberg writes of the violence, past and present, that shapes the people of the vast American Midwest. Deep and searing, *Blue Earth* is perhaps one of the best novels of the past decade."

—Kathleen Spivack, author of *With Robert Lowell and His Circle*

paperback * hardcover * eBook

ISBN 978-1-61599-146-4

www.ModernHistoryPress.com

CPSIA information can be obtained
at www.ICGtesting.com
Printed in the USA
BVHW040144190720
R10975800001B/R109758PG583614BVX11B/1

9 781615 995189